Raven the Great
What is Junetheeth?

All rights reserved. No part of this book may be reproduced, stored
in a retrieval system, or transmitted in any form, by any means,
including mechanical, electronic, photocopying, recording, or
otherwise, without the prior written permission of the author.

Copyright 2020 Paulette McClain
ISBN 978-0-578-74661-6
www.kp-publishing.com

Published and printed in the United States of America

Book Design and Layout
Labyrinthe Design Group

ACKNOWLEDGMENTS

I'm so thankful for the inspiration to bring this project to fruition. For my sister Shampella - I hope this makes you smile. I'm also deeply grateful to have the support of my husband, family, and dear friends who cheer me on.

Thank you all for your unwavering support and love.

Momma and Daddy - your baby girl is still at it. Your prayers continue to keep, lift, and propel me forward.

For our Raven

God blessed us with your presence for only a short while and you left us without our saying goodbye. I write to feel your presence and to keep you close. Thank you for teaching us to laugh and for opening our eyes to see ourselves. I also thank you for teaching us to accept each other's differences. Now that you're resting, I know that your mind is at peace. I'll write in remembrance of you. I want the world to know how special you were.

Until our meeting in the air, I love you.

-Tee Paulette

Dr. Paulette McClain

Illustrated by: Anthony D. Carson

The alarm rings and as always it was the most annoying sound.

"RAVEN, GET UP, AND COME EAT!
"BREAKFAST IS ON THE TABLE!!!",
her mother yells from down the hall.

"Awwhh Man..... Already?" Raven moans as she yawns and turns off her favorite childhood cartoon character alarm clock.

She immediately opens her eyes, as she remembers what today was - Black History Presentation Day!!

Raven was prepared, excited and ready to get to school for her big day.

"Good morning, my name is Rae Rae,
I mean Raven, and my topic...."

Just then, her mother opens
the door, this time with much
more seriousness in her voice
and now holding her husband's
best Sunday belt in her left
hand.

"If I have to tell you one more time to
come out of this room to eat, it's going
to be me and you young lady!"

"Yes ma'am, I was just practicing for
my presentation", Raven explained.

Come on baby girl. Tell us about it
after breakfast", her mom welcomed.

When arriving to the kitchen, Raven was excited to find that her grandparents were over for a visit and their morning coffee.

"Good morning Maw Maw and Paw Paw!" Raven announced when entering.

"Good morning my baaaby, Raven's grandmother said, while opening her arms for a hug.

"There she is- Look at our Rae Rae!!!" her grandfather announced. "Girl, you're almost as tall as me!" Raven's grandpa always made her feel taller than their previous visit.

After sitting, Raven said her grace and started eating.

"Ya'll wanna hear my presentation? It's black history presentation day, and I'm reporting about Juneteenth!" she exclaimed excitingly.

Her grandmother, sounding overcome with pride,
"Now, that a girl! Tell them about our history! I bet those teachers
down there don't teach you that in school", she ended.

After taking a few more bites, Raven sipped her orange
juice and she stood up.   She cleared her throat and started,

"Good morning class! My name is Raven",
all the while looking downward.

"No ma'am!! Lift your head and stand tall!
You speak boldly young lady", her grandmother coached.

Raven started over, this time standing a bit taller, and sounding
more confident. Raven's family looked on with pride.

A few moments later, there was a loud honk from a car outside. Raven's aunt had arrived to take her to school.

It was Aunt PJ's day to get Raven and her cousins to school. Raven loved riding to school with her aunt. She loved their talks and the car games that she and her cousins would play on their way to school.

"Good morning Rae Rae!" her aunt welcomed as Raven hopped in on the front passenger side and kissed her aunt on the cheek.

"Good morning Tee", she added. It was Raven's turn to sit up front, and she wanted to rub it in. "Good morning ya'll! She announced as if she were singing while gazing at them teasingly.

On the ride to school, all Raven could think about was how she might do with presenting. She was a bit uneasy with speaking in front of the class, so she asked her aunt,
"What do I do if my classmates laugh at me?

Her aunt looked over to her while driving with adoration.
"Little girl, first let me tell you that you have half the battle won - you're beautiful and people like to look at good looking folks!"

Raven smiled. Her aunt shared that she too had the same fear while growing up, and gave her the best advice anyone could ask for.

"You have to keep in mind that most people don't know, and you have to tell it. And if you're afraid to do so, then who will?" Raven gazed away, and glanced back at her aunt.

"Well I never thought of it that way Tee PJ, that helps, thanks."

"Now go crush it little girl!!" her aunt encouraged, while giving Raven a fist bump.

Later that day, the fourth grade students hustled to their seats before the second bell. Everyone dressed neatly in their uniforms, but all wearing them slightly differently to match their personalities.

Mrs. Sowell stood from her desk and welcomed the class,
"Good afternoon everyone!

I'm sure you're all excited and prepared to report this afternoon. I've invited Mrs. Wilson's second grade class to join us, and they're excited to hear what you have prepared."
Raven could feel herself getting nervous,
but then thought about the helpful tip that her aunt shared.

Soon Mrs. Wilson's students entered the class in the straightest of single file lines (Mrs. Wilson didn't play, and the kids knew to be on their best behavior), one of Raven's classmates Sammy leaned over to her and whispered, "I wanna go first to get this over with."

Mrs. Sowell chose to call the students alphabetically, which meant that after Clara Aucoin, it was Paul Batiste's turn to report.

Paul had the attention of everyone, and his classmates knew that he probably didn't finish his report, but he had the gift of filibustering. He was to report about Lewis Latimar, but spent most of his time talking about how Thomas Edison stole Mr. Latimar's invention.

Paul was near the end of his report, when he poured it on "…. and as one of the top students of my class, I'd like to add that it was quite a pleasure to research this information and to stand before you today - Thank you!", he ended.

Just then, Mrs. Sowell suggested, "Please share your sources with us Paul", while giving him a firm look. "Um, um…. Wikipedia, my grandmother's encyclopedias, and Google," Paul shared.

Just then one of the second graders asked, "What's an encyclopedia?" Raven and her classmates started giggling. "You may have a seat Paul", Mrs. Sowell suggested. "…And see me after class", she added swiftly. The class erupted with whispers and giggles. Mrs. Sowell quickly stood and commanded the attention of the class again.

"Next, we will hear from Raven",
she stated as she took her seat again.

Raven took a deep breath, stood, and walked to the front of the class. As she made her way to the front of the class, she thought about the pep talk from her aunt and whispered to herself, "It's my job to tell it, I can do this!" As she turned to face the class, she looked around at all the blank stares, took another deep breath and belted,

"GOOD MORNING EVERYBODY,
I'm Raven Fontenot!"

Just then she looked over at Sammy, and realized he was holding her prop with a mischievous look on his face. Raven started to break a sweat. "Excuse me, I forgot my poster", she said as she whisked over to Sammy's desk to lightly pry it out of his fingers "Thank you Sam", she said while clinching her teeth, and rolling her eyes.

As she quickly moved back to her place,
she held her artistically made sign high, and started,

"WHAT IS JUNETEENTH?"

Raven continued, "Juneteenth is the one of oldest nationally celebrated holidays in America, which commemorates the freedom of slaves."

Before Raven could get out another word, one of the second graders raised her hand and volunteered, "I've never heard of Juneteenth!" Raven's classmate Sarah added, ". . . and we don't celebrate that holiday!"

Raven glared at Sarah, "Thank you for making my point! Most people don't celebrate it, because they don't know about it." So, listen up, and you might learn something!" Raven continued, as she rolled her eyes.

Mrs. Sowell giggled to herself. "Go on Raven, "she prompted.

"As I was saying, Juneteenth, short for June 19th,
is the day back in 1865 that Major General Granger
and his soldiers marched into Galveston, Texas to give the great
news that the slaves were free." Raven explained.

"But before we get to June 19th, you have to know that in
1863 the Civil War was fought, and in the largest battle of that war-
The Battle of Gettysburg,
Union troops waxed …. I mean they beat the Confederate troops."

Raven went on to share such a vivid story about how that victory
led to President Abraham Lincoln writing the Emancipation
Proclamation.

"What's an Eman-ca-paction?",
one of the second graders asked.

Raven giggled and answered,
"The Emancipation Proclamation was an executive order written
to emancipate slaves in the 11 Confederate states who were at war
against the union, which allowed slaves to help in the fight against
the Confederate soldiers."

Paul raised his hand, "So if the President signed an order to free
slaves in confederate states - Texas being one of them, in 1863, why
did the slaves in Texas find out over two years later?"

"Good question my smart friend", Raven answered.

"They should've just called and told them," another kid answered.

"Now look ya'll - remember that they didn't have cellphones back
then", Raven started laughing and the class joined in.

Mrs. Sowell and Mrs. Wilson also joined in on the laughter.

"There are many stories as to why slaves in Texas were the last to know they were free." Raven exclaimed.

"Some believed that the government and slave owners wanted to get more work out of them before they found out they were free", she added.

"That's mean!", a kid on the back row expressed.

"Well slave owners were not nice idiots!", Sammy expressed.

Mrs. Sowell glared at Sammy,
"Do you want detention young man?" she asked.

Five minutes later, Raven was ending her presentation.

"Juneteenth started as a holiday celebrated in Texas, but is now nationally recognized. Ya'll also need to know that it took a constitutional amendment-The 13th Amendment, written in 1865 to finally end the institution of slavery for good . So ya'll read more about the holiday, and ask your parents about ways to celebrate it.
Thank you!"

The students and teachers all applauded.

As Raven returned to her seat, Sammy asked Mrs. Sowell,
"Did you know about Juneteenth?"
Mrs. Sowell smiled, "Why sure I did." she answered.
"Well why don't you teach us about it?"

Mrs. Sowell followed, "Your curriculum doesn't include that as a
topic, so I include activities such as this,
to give you an opportunity to learn about it".
She then met eye contact with Mrs. Wilson and they smiled.

"Good job Rae Rae!!" Sammy congratulated Raven.
She was so excited to have done so well. She could hardly wait
to go home to share with her family how she had done.

The bell rang moments later and
it was time to head to the car pool line.

As they entered the hallway to head to the carpool line, Paul
motioned to Raven, "I should've gotten you to write my report",
he whispered. "It's not too late, because you're gonna have to do
yours over anyway," They both giggled.

Raven's grandmother was first in the carpool line. Several steps before reaching the car, Raven could hear her grandmother's favorite blues song playing. Smiling and starting to sway to the music, she turned to wave to her friends before jumping into the vehicle and greeting her grandmother.

"Hey maw maw, guess what? I did real good - I know I got an A!"
That's my Rae Rae, her grandmother proudly answered.

Her cousins soon loaded into the car, greeted their grandmother, and soon they were on their way.

During the ride home, Raven gazed out of the window and thought about her accomplishment. She had done just what her aunt encouraged her to do, she told the story.

She smiled as she heard her grandmother snapping her fingers and singing. Raven joined in singing the song, "Ah shucks, ah shucks, my, my, my, my baby, she's doing me wrong…"

Raven closed her eyes as she swayed and sang. She allowed the sunshine to warm her face.

It was a great day!

The Author

In memory of her beloved niece Raven, Dr. Paulette McClain, a Louisiana native, introduces to children the importance of African-American history. As a Nurse Educator for over 20 years and Nurse Practitioner, Dr. McClain is dedicating time to educate in a different way by teaching children history through stories inspired by memories of her adorable niece Raven (affectionately remembered as Rae Rae).

As a wife and mother of two young adults, who stressed the importance of reading, she wishes to inspire children to learn more about historical events and topics that they may not learn about in school. Dr. McClain also wishes to share great stories that might create meaningful moments for both children and their parents.

Made in the USA
Coppell, TX
14 June 2021

57412285R00024